Dear mouse friends,
Welcome to the world of

Geronimo Stilton

THE RODENT'S GAZETTE
EDITORIAL STAFF

Geronimo Stilton
A learned and brainy
mouse; editor of
The Rodent's Gazette

Thea Stilton
Geronimo's sister and
special correspondent at
The Rodent's Gazette

Trap Stilton
An awful joker;
Geronimo's cousin and
owner of the store
Cheap Junk for Less

Benjamin Stilton
A sweet and loving
nine-year-old mouse;
Geronimo's favorite
nephew

Geronimo Stilton

THE CHOCOLATE CHASE

Scholastic Inc.

Copyright © 2016 by Edizioni Piemme S.p.A., Palazzo Mondadori, Via Mondadori 1, 20090 Segrate, Italy. International Rights © Atlantyca S.p.A. English translation © 2017 by Atlantyca S.p.A.

The publisher does not have any control over and does not assume any responsibility for author or third-party websites or their content.

GERONIMO STILTON names, characters, and related indicia are copyright, trademark, and exclusive license of Atlantyca S.p.A. All rights reserved. The moral right of the author has been asserted. Based on an original idea by Elisabetta Dami. www.geronimostilton.com

Published by Scholastic Inc., *Publishers since 1920*, 557 Broadway, New York, NY 10012. SCHOLASTIC and associated logos are trademarks and/or registered trademarks of Scholastic Inc.

Stilton is the name of a famous English cheese. It is a registered trademark of the Stilton Cheese Makers' Association. For more information, go to www.stiltoncheese.com.

ISBN 978-1-338-15915-8

Text by Geronimo Stilton
Original title *Lo strano caso del ladro di cioccolato*
Cover by Danilo Barozzi
Illustrations by Danilo Loizedda (design), Antonio Campo (pencils), and Daria Cerchi and Serena Gianoli (color)
Graphics by Michela Battaglin

Special thanks to Anna Bloom
Translated by Anna Pizzelli
Interior design by Kevin Callahan/BNGO Books

10 9 8 7 6 5 4 3 2 1   17 18 19 20 21

Printed in the U.S.A.   40

First printing 2017

READY FOR ANYTHING!

I stood on the roof of the Rodent's Gazette office building and admired the view. Little birds chirped from flowered branches, the breeze blew softly through my whiskers, and the Sun was shining brightly.

What a perfect day for New Mouse City's annual Spring Festival! Everymouse looked forward to celebrating the end of winter and spending time with friends and family. There were fun activities scheduled all over town.

What a mouserific day!

But first, it was my turn to take care of our newspaper's vegetable garden.

I was watering the plants, when a sudden loud voice scared the cheddar out of me.

"Mr. Stilton!" my assistant, Mousella, cried. "What are you still doing up here? It's very late!"

"Moldy mozzarella!" I squeaked. "Don't sneak up on me like that!" I leaned over to GRAB the rake I'd left on the ground. But I stepped on the end and —

Mr. Stilton! It's late!

What?

BAAAAANG!

The handle hit me smack in the middle of my snout! Ouch!

I saw cheese stars! I stumbled across the roof, holding my head in my paws.

"Mr. Stilton, watch out for the fertilizer . . ." Mousella cried.

But it was too late! I fell tail first right into the smelly fertilizer.

This was not a good look for me. I am *Geronimo Stilton*, editor in chief of the Rodent's Gazette, the most famouse **NEWSPAPER** on Mouse Island!

At least the *Rodent's Gazette*'s garden looked fabumouse. We're very proud of it. We grow flowers, VEGETABLES, and a few small citrus trees. We even have some beehives to produce delicious honey.

"I hope you have a change of clothing, Mr. Stilton." Mousella sighed. "That fertilizer smells like **rotten Gorgonzola**!"

"Of course! Today I am ready for anything!"

"Are you sure?" Mousella asked.

"Today is the Spring Festival. The Rodent's Gazette needs all paws on deck to cover every moment for our readers! Are you coming? Do you have your flyer?"

"But that's why I **came up** here, Mr. Stilton. You're late for your staff meeting!"

Squeak, what a disaster!

"I tried calling. Is your cell phone off?"

"Holey Swiss cheese, you're right!" I cried, pulling my phone out of my

Spring Festival

DON'T MISS . . .
· The Baking Competition
· The Mousebergé Egg Exhibit
· The Egg Hunt

In New Mouse City, everyone celebrates spring by giving one another yummy chocolate eggs.

pocket. It had been off the whole morning! I tried dusting some of the fertilizer from my dirty clothes. "I'll just have to go like this. Come on!"

It was my meeting—they couldn't start without me!

A VERY LONG DAY

As soon as I arrived at the staff meeting, everyone started complaining about a smell.

"Who brought the rancid rat snack?"

"Quick, open the windows!"

I tried to back out of the room before anyone noticed I was the source of the smell, but my cousin Trap **burst** through the door and halted my escape.

"Geronimeister, what a mess. What, did you fall in some **fertilizer**?"

"SHHH!" I whispered, but it was too late.

"You're right, Trap! Mr. Stilton did fall in the fertilizer!" Mousella said.

The whole room turned to stare at me. I blushed. **Great gobs of gooey cheese**, how embarrassing!

Trap *quickly* distracted everymouse by telling some stinky PUNS.

Then he dragged me to my office, closing the door behind him.

In my office, I changed into clean clothes. I went through a list of things I needed to do.

"First, I have to get back to the editorial meeting," I said to myself. "Then I **have to go visit** the Mousebergé Egg Exhibit

This is so embarrassing!

so I can write an article about it —"

"You don't have time for that!" Trap interrupted me. "You PROMISED to help me with the baking **competition**!"

"What? I don't remember that," I said.

"But I need you," Trap cried. "You have an exceptional SNOUT for chocolate!"

I sighed. "I'm sorry, Trap. I have too many things to take care of today."

Just then my **COMPUTER** started shrieking.

"Geronimooooooo!"

I jumped in surprise. *"Greasy Gorgonzola!* What is that?"

Trap chuckled. "Geronimo, you are such a **scaredy-mouse**! It's just Hercule Poirat, video conferencing you on your computer!"

I **LOOKED** down at my computer. Trap was right. The snout of my friend, private detective Hercule Poirat, was **staring** back at me!

"Hercule, what in the FROZEN FETA are you doing on my computer screen?" I asked.

"Hello, Geronimo," he said. "Do not fear, I have installed a little program on your computer so that we can video-chat whenever I want!"

I smoothed my whiskers and waited for my heart to stop POUNDING out of my chest.

"Now I can call you anytime I need to ask for your **HELP**!" Hercule continued.

"Speaking of help," Trap said. "Hercule, convince him he has to help me win the BAKING COMPETITION!"

I opened my mouth to explain why I couldn't, but Hercule jumped in. "Trap is your cousin! You have to **HELP** him!"

I was outnumbered. "Okay, Trap. I will help you. I'll meet you at your **kitchen** as soon as my editorial meeting is over."

Trap was so happy he started dancing the **samba** and singing, "Great, great, great **cousinkins** . . . you deserve a **mega-hug**. I knew I could count on you!"

Trap **danced** right out the door, and I turned back to my computer.

Hercule cleared his throat. "Since you're

in a helping mood, how do you feel about helping me, too?"

Thundering cat tails, I could not say no to a friend in need! Even when I had so much to do already . . .

"You can count on me, Hercule. I'll come by your office before I go see Trap."

Hercule gave me a THUMBS-UP and signed off from the video chat.

Geronimo, how do you feel about helping me?

I sighed. I had promised to help both Trap and **HERCULE** — and I still needed to get to the egg exhibit. This was going to be a VERY LONG day!

EVERYTHING IS UNDER CONTROL!

I took a deep breath, checked to make sure my shirt was tucked in, and started WALKING toward the meeting room. Mousella stood in front of the door.

So much to do!

"Mr. Stilton, we are already behind schedule!" she squeaked. Then she paused, looking at my face. "You seem tired — is everything okay?"

"I am just fine!" I huffed. "Everything is under control. I just have a lot of cheese on my plate today. I promised Hercule I would help him with a SECRET matter, and then I have to help Trap bake his **CHOCOLATE EGG**, and then . . ." I trailed off.

Mousella held up her paw. "No worries, I have taken care of everything!"

She tapped something on her tablet and pulled up a list of all the *Spring Festival* events. She had gone through and assigned every staff rodent an event to cover for the festival special issue.

I looked at her in surprise. I didn't have to lift a paw! "Mousella, thank you so much! I don't know what I would do without you. Since you have this covered, can you call me a TAXI, please? I have to go to Hercule's office, ASAP!"

"Mr. Stilton, it's the *Spring Festival*—all of the streets are blocked off. The whole city is traffic-free today! You won't be able to find a taxi in all of New Mouse City!"

Toasted cheese sandwiches! I had completely forgotten! My heart sank and I turned as white as a slice of MOZZARELLA CHEESE. I was never going to be able to do everything on my list now. There simply won't be enough time!

Mousella's face suddenly brightened. "I have a great idea! Why don't you rent a bike instead? There's a bike-share kiosk just around the corner."

Why not rent a bike?

"That is a great idea!" I said, very relieved.

"You just need one thing first," Mousella said. She ran back to my office and returned with my helmet.

"Have a great bike ride, Mr. Stilton!" she cried.

BIKE SHARING

Bike-sharing services provide bicycles for people to rent. This encourages people to drive less, which can help decrease traffic congestion and air pollution. In New Mouse City, the bike stations are located in every neighborhood, close to public transportation stops and parks.

ONE LAZY MOUSE

Just as Mousella had said, there was a bike-share **station** right next to the Rodent's Gazette office. A row of bicycles stood lined up next to what looked like an ATM.

I jiggled a bike, but it seemed to be locked into the kiosk. "Now how do I rent one?" I wondered out loud.

"Insert your credit card in the slot!" a funny voice called out.

"Oh, thank you," I said, turning around. I stopped in surprise. There was no one there! "Hello?" I tried.

The funny voice spoke again. "Insert your credit card!"

I still couldn't see a single rodent! How

was that possible?

"BIKE station number three-seven-three-seven! Insert your card!" the voice demanded.

I slapped my forehead. I was a very silly mouse—the voice was coming from inside the thing that looked like an ATM!

Hello?

Bike station number 3-7-3-7!

This was how I rented a bike! I inserted my credit card in the slot.

The metallic-sounding voice started up again. "Thanks for choosing New Mouse City Bike Share. Bike sharing helps lower city traffic and pollution and promotes a healthy, active lifestyle. Please enter your name."

I typed my name into the keypad and waited for more instructions. Soon, a list of biker-achievement levels popped up on the screen.

"Geronimo Stilton!" the computer chimed. "Welcome. Your biker level is **Lazy Biker**!

"How dare you!" I cried.

I didn't want to be labeled a "Lazy Biker" even if it was my first time. I tapped on the keypad. "How do I GO UP one level?" I

SUPER-MEGA-STRONG BIKER:
BIKES ALL DAY, EVERY DAY

SUPER-MEGA BIKER: BIKES DAILY

STRONG BIKER: BIKES A FEW
TIMES A WEEK

SATISFACTORY BIKER: BIKES ONCE
A WEEK

VERY LAZY BIKER: BIKES ONCE
A MONTH

HOPELESS BIKER: BIKES ONCE
A YEAR

LAZY BIKER: FIRST-TIME BIKER

wondered out loud. Hopeless seemed a little
better, at least!

The computer beeped. "To increase your
level, please activate a ten-year membership,
payable in full, immediately."

"Yes, yes, that's fine as long as you release
a bicycle!" I tapped the necessary keys.

"Membership now active!"

the computer cheered. "Congratulations, Geronimo Stilton, you are the first one to buy the SUPER-MEGA-DELUXE membership!"

Then the kiosk ejected my credit card and . . . a very long receipt!

The super-mega-deluxe membership was **expensive**! I tried not to think of all the cheese I could have bought with that money. I put on my **HELMET**, picked out a bike, and started *pedaling* as fast as I could!

I'm late!

An Eggnapping!

I *biked* and *biked* and *biked* until I felt like melted mozzarella. I hadn't realized I was so out of shape! This day had barely started and I already needed a nap.

After what seemed like forever, Hercule's office finally came into view. He worked just outside New Mouse City's PORT.

Gasp!

I turned left and took a deep inhale. But instead of a lungful of fresh, salty air, I breathed in something much yummier. Holey cheese, it was one of my favorite **desserts**, cheddar vanilla scones! Maybe I should follow that smell . . .

But just then my cell phone **rang** and I almost tipped my bike over in **SURPRISE**. I pedaled to the side of the road and answered the call.

Hercule's voice boomed out at me. "What's taking you so long, Geronimo? I'm here waiting for you! And I need your H E L P!"

"Be there soon!" I squeaked.

Not far away, I spotted a bike station just like the one near my office. I quickly placed the bike in the rack. I could check out another bike after I visited Hercule. Then I hastily smoothed down my fur and headed to Hercule's office.

I **KNOCKED** and waited to be let in.

"Password please!" a voice called through the door.

"Come on, Hercule, it's **ME**!" I said.

"Me who?" the voice asked.

"Geronimo Stilton! You asked me to come!"

The door opened and **HERCULE** looked annoyed. "You should have said it was you right away. We have no time to lose on SILLY games!"

He waved me in and closed the door firmly behind me.

As usual, Hercule's office was a total **mess**. How did he find anything in here?

Just the sight of so many piles of stuff made me itchy all over. I scratched my elbow and

Gross!

looked for a place to sit. An old armchair seemed like the best bet, but it obviously hadn't been cleaned in a very long time. It smelled worse than a **MOLDY WHEEL OF BRIE**.

I took a step forward to investigate further, but my paw landed on something **slippery** and went right out from under me!

WHOOSH!

I went tail over ears and landed in a heap in front of Hercule's desk.

"Hercule, this office could really use a **DEEP CLEAN**, don't you think?" I asked.

My friend shook his snout. "No time for that, my friend! We've got more **important** things to discuss."

"Sure," I muttered, picking myself up and removing a **banana peel** from under my paw. "What's the urgent matter that you needed my **help** with?"

"I'm glad you asked!" Hercule

SQUEAKED. "Did you see your sister, **THEA**, yesterday? Did she say anything about me? I sent her a basket of homegrown bananas."

Cheese niblets! "Are you telling me that I biked all the way out here just so you could ask me about Thea?!"

Hercule looked offended. "I just wanted to know if she mentioned me. Those bananas are not so easy to grow. It's an entire tree!"

I put my snout in my paws. "No, she didn't. And if that's all you needed to talk about, I really should be going." I turned to leave.

"Well, I guess that means you don't want to help me find the world famous *Mousebergé Egg*!"

I stopped in my tracks. "The Mousebergé Egg? Isn't it at the mouseum? It's the main highlight of the **egg exhibit**, which opens tonight. The unveiling is the most important event of this year's *Spring Festival*. I'm supposed to write an article about it!"

"It's been **eggnapped**!" Hercule exclaimed. "We have to find it before the exhibit opens tonight — or the whole *Spring Festival* will be ruined!"

"*Rancid ricotta!* The egg has been

MOUSEBERGÉ EGG

Mousebergé is one of the most famouse jewelers of all time. He traveled the world to learn all the best techniques. One of his trips took him to New Mouse City during the first Spring Festival. When he received a chocolate egg as a present from a young mouselet, he decided to return the kindness with a very special egg. It was crafted from solid gold and decorated with rubies, sapphires, and emeralds.

He had so much fun creating this egg that legend has it he made seven more exactly like it. But now only one of these amazing eggs is left: the first, created during New Mouse City's original Spring Festival!

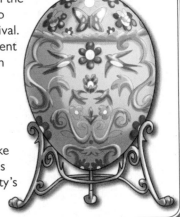

stolen? This is a cat-astrophe!" I pulled at my whiskers. "Why did you have me come all the way here? We should have met at the museum to save time."

Hercule shrugged. "You are the one who said you would meet me here. You were in such a hurry to go that I didn't have a chance to explain. Besides, today the **streets are BLOCKED OFF**, remember? I need a ride!"

BICYCLE BUILT FOR TWO!

Hercule and I raced out to the bike-share station. Fortunately, they had several tandem bicycles that two **mice** could ride at the same time. Just what we **needed**!

But when I tried to unlock one of the TANDEM bicycles from the rack, the little voice from inside the kiosk stopped me. "To rent a tandem bicycle, please pay the additional charge!" it chimed.

"What?" I cried.

Sigh!

"I just paid for a super-mega-deluxe membership!!! Isn't everything included?"

"No! Please insert your credit card in the slot!"

CRUSTY CHEESE CURDS! I inserted my credit card again, paid another fee, and watched the kiosk spit out another very long receipt.

Finally, Hercule and I were on our way to the mouseum. With two of us pedaling, the trip should have been as easy as **cheesy pie!**

In no time, however, I was **EXHAUSTED**. At a traffic light, I turned to see if Hercule was as tired as I was. But I saw that he was reading the **NEWSPAPER**! His paws weren't even touching the pedals!

"Hercule! What are you doing back there?"

"I have to conserve my energy for

MYSTERY solving, of course," he said. "Oh, look, the light just turned GREEN. We better get going!"

I sighed and started pedaling AGAIN.

As soon as we reached the mouseum, I jammed on the brakes . . . and sprawled over the handlebars.

"Leave me here," I panted. "I'm as fried as a day-old mozzarella stick."

I'm so tired!

"Nonsense," Hercule cried. "Look alive, Geronimo, here comes Grant von Paintmouse, the mouseum director."

Grant von Paintmouse

"Here you are, finally! Follow me!" the frantic-looking director said, waving us forward.

I staggered to my paws and returned the bicycle to the nearest station. I leaned it against an empty wall and hurried to catch up with Hercule and the director.

As we entered the main hall, where the egg exhibit had been set up, I looked around curiously. "Wasn't anyone guarding the Mousebergé Egg?"

"Of course someone was," Grant said.

"But the **CHEDDARHEAD** fell asleep on the job! The thieves stole the egg right out from under his **whiskers**."

We had reached the display case where the Mousebergé Egg had been. I could smell a strange, sweet scent in the air. It reminded me of something—but I couldn't quite put my PAW on what it was.

The director pointed at where a perfect oval hole had been cut out of the glass. The oval still rested on the floor. Hercule pulled out his detective **MAGNIFYING GLASS** and looked over the scene of the crime carefully.

"Geronimo, take a **picture** of me with your PHONE," Hercule said.

"Did you find a clue you need documented?" I asked eagerly.

"Nope, nothing yet! I just want Thea

to see how *handsome* I look when I'm investigating a case!"

Moldy mozzarella! "Hercule, is this really the right time for that? We have to find the missing egg!" I gestured to the empty display case.

But before I could say anything else, my cell phone flew out of my outstretched

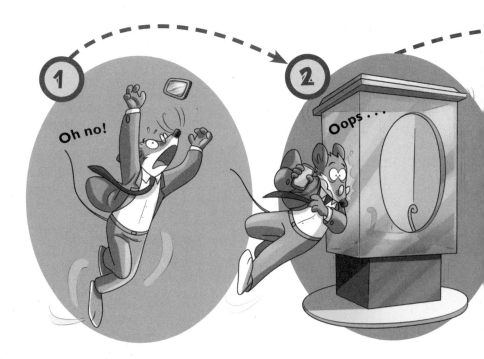

paw. To catch it before it hit the ground, **(1)** I lunged forward, **(2) BUMPED into** the display case, and **(3)** smashed my snout against the **MARBLE** stand!

"**Yikes!** Are you okay?" the director asked. "This display case is made with a special material. It's unbreakable, indestructible, and crushproof.

Hercule shook his snout in disbelief. "But the **THIEF** was able to cut a hole right through it!"

The director rubbed his whiskers. "He must have used a very pure diamond, then! It's the only thing that could even scratch this special material!"

"Hmmm," Hercule said. "That's our first clue, then!"

"And I just found our second one!" I cried from the ground. "Look!"

The two of them glanced down to see what I had found. I held up a long BLOND hair that had gotten caught at the base of the stand.

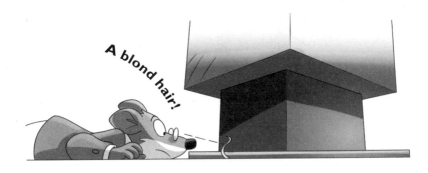

A blond hair!

"Cheesy toast crumbs! Well done, Geronimo! Our thief has LONG BLOND HAIR and access to a very pure DIAMOND! We've practically got this thing solved!" Hercule cried.

"It's a start, at least," I said. "It's not easy to get your paws on a very pure **diamond** ... we need to talk to an expert!"

Just then my cell phone RANG.

Hercule's eyes lit up like he'd just spotted a **cheese plate**. "Is that Thea? Tell her I say hello."

I rolled my eyes. "It's Creepella," I said, before accepting the call. *"Hello, Creepella, how are you?"*

"Geronimo, where are you?" she shouted. "ARE YOU COMING TO THE EGG HUNT?"

"I'm busy now. I need to find a diamond expert for a top secret project," I said.

Creepella squeaked. "Oh, Geronimo, you don't have to be secretive—I can tell you're looking for a birthday gift for me!"

I gulped. "No, Creepella, that's not it at all. It's for something else . . . SOMETHING SECRET . . ."

"Whatever you say, Geronimo," Creepella said. "For this **secret matter**, you should visit the best jewelry store in town, Mousetacular Jewels. Talk to Mousieur von Gold. He is the best—he'll

Creepella is Geronimo's friend. She has expensive taste!

know just what I'll like."

I groaned. "Sorry, Creepella, I think we have a bad phone connection — gotta go!"

I turned back to Hercule. But before I could say anything, my phone **beeped** again.

"Maybe this is Thea!" Hercule cried.

"It's just a text from Trap," I said. "I have to go see him. But Creepella said we could find a jewelry expert at Mousetacular Jewels. You go there, and I'll meet you as soon as I can."

> Geronimo, where are you? Don't let me down. Come right away!!!

TASTE TEST

I grabbed my helmet and hopped on a new bike and started pedaling my way to Trap.

The city streets were **crowded** by now. Families strolled along enjoying **ICE CREAM** and flying kites. A long line of mouselets had already formed for the egg hunt.

What a fabumouse day!

Suddenly, my cell phone started beeping again. I tried to ignore it so I could focus on biking, but it kept ringing! Who could it be now?

I pulled over to the

side of the road to take a look. I had several urgent messages from my reporters about their *Spring Festival* articles. I was in a hurry, but I couldn't help myself, I replied to all of them.

With that taken care of, I started pedaling furiously again. I **PROMISED** Trap I would help him — I couldn't let him down!

Argh!

When I arrived at the **Grand Hotel,** my lower paws hurt because of all the biking, and my upper paws hurt because of all the **typing**!

How was I going to be able to help both Trap and Hercule at the same time, especially with sore paws?

Wearily, I stowed my bike at the bike-share station outside the hotel. I would just have to explain to Trap that I was in no shape to be his **taster**.

Inside the hotel, I headed down to the kitchen, where Trap was working. I had barely gotten through the kitchen doors when Trap pounced on me and shoved a **chocolate** bar under my snout.

"You're here! Quick, try this super-spicy chocolate I made! I think it's perfect for my chocolate egg." I took a small bite, but Trap didn't wait for my reaction.

"Maybe I should use this lemon chocolate, instead? Or the garlic chocolate!" Trap kept forcing me to taste **crazier** and **crazier** flavors of chocolate until, finally, I couldn't eat another bite!

53

FLAVOR #4
Almond chocolate . . .
ALMOST BROKE A TOOTH!
FLAVOR #5
Cheesy chocolate . . .
TOO STICKY!
FLAVOR #6
Carrot chocolate . . .
DISGUSTING!
FLAVOR #7
Lemon chocolate . . .
TOO SOUR!
FLAVOR #8
Lettuce chocolate . . .
GAVE ME A HEADACHE!

"Which one did you like best, Geronimo? The GARLIC? LETTUCE? Or maybe the LEMON?"

I'm very nauseous!

But my mouth was still **full** of chocolate and I felt slightly **sick** to my stomach. I feebly waved my paw at him.

"Oh, I see," Trap cried. "They were all so amaze-mouse that you're speechless! That's **mouserific**—I will use all ten flavors in my egg!"

I put my snout in my paws. That was going to be one strange egg!

Trap looked around at his workstation. "Hmm, I seem to be out of almonds," he said.

"I'll go get some for you," I said. This was my opportunity to get back to HERCULE.

Before Trap could disagree, I **DAſHED** back out of the kitchen. There was no time to lose!

Trap's chocolate churned in my stomach as I pedaled. I hoped that he wouldn't come up with any more WEIRD flavors while I was gone.

A Fabumouse Ring

In no time, I screeched to a halt outside Mousetacular Jewels. Hercule was there waiting for me.

"Geronimo! What took you so long? Let's go inside!"

I stashed my bike outside the shop and we stepped through the front doors. I was immediately blinded by the incredimouse sparkle of thousands of jewels.

A sales-mouselet scurried up and handed me a pair of SUNGLASSES. "These will protect your eyes while you admire our **mousetacular** jewelry!" he said.

The sales-mouselet went back to his post, and a very **elegantly** dressed mouse approached us.

"Welcome! I am Mousieur von Gold. You must be Mr. Stilton. Ms. von Cacklefur already called me. I know just what you're looking for!"

"Actually . . . there's something else you could HELP me with first," I said. "By any chance have you recently sold an extremely pure DiAMOND to a mouselet with long blond hair?"

Mousieur von Gold shook his snout. "No, not to a blond mouselet. However, yesterday a mouselet with very short dark hair asked to look at the purest **diamond** ring we had for sale."

HERCULE leaned in eagerly. "Did she buy it?"

"No, she didn't," he said. "I can show it to you now. In fact, it would make the perfect birthday present — I'm sure Ms. von Cacklefur would **love** it!"

I gulped and we followed Mousieur von Gold over to the counter where the special jewel was kept.

Mousieur von Gold opened the LITTLE box containing the diamond **RING**, and turned whiter than a slice of mozzarella cheese!

"Nooo!" he cried. "This . . . this is not

Hmmmm . . .

A mouselet with short, dark hair . . .

the real **diamond**! It does not sparkle! IT'S . . . IT'S . . . IT'S AN ORDINARY PIECE OF GLASS!"

Hercule and I exchanged a knowing glance.

"The mouse with the short **HAIR** must have swapped the diamonds when you showed the **RING** to her," I said.

"And then she used it to cut through the glass case at the museum and steal the **MOUSEBERGÉ EGG**!" Hercule added. He stroked his whiskers thoughtfully.

"Do you remember anything else about that **MOUSELET**?" I asked.

Mousieur von Gold collapsed into a nearby chair. "She asked me if there was a pharmacy close by. I told her there was one in the organic grocery store around the corner." He paused. "I also remember that she was wearing a very expensive-smelling **perfume**."

"**Perfume?**" I repeated.

"Yes, it was some kind of cheddar-vanilla fragrance," Mousieur von Gold said.

His description REMINDED me of something . . . but I wasn't sure what it was.

Hercule had heard enough.

Oh dear!

"Let's go check out that organic grocery store, Geronimo," he said.

We thanked Mousieur von Gold, returned our SUNGLASSES, and headed out the door.

THE SCENT OF CHEDDAR VANILLA

As we walked to the organic grocery store at the end of the block, my phone beeped again. A newspaper editor's job is never done! I tapped a few responses to reporters' questions.

Hmmm . . .

ORGANIC GROCERY STORE

I was so absorbed in my phone that I wasn't paying much attention to where I was walking.

BAM!

I bumped right into the grocery store's front door!

CRASH!

I fell snoutfirst onto the ground. My head spun.

Hercule laughed. "You can be so absentminded, Geronimo! You're going to have a big bump on your snout tomorrow."

He helped me up and we stepped into the store.

Luckily, there were no customers, so we were able to ask the manager mouse a few questions.

"Have you seen an elegant mouse with short dark hair recently?" I asked.

Have you seen an elegant mouse with short dark hair?

Hmm, no.

"Hmm, no!" The manager mouse said.

"What about a *mouselet* with long blond HAIR?" Hercule asked.

"Nope, I don't remember a mouselet like that, either."

I could tell Hercule felt as *discouraged* as I did. Was this a **dead end**?

"Well, have you seen any unusual mice at all in the last few days?" Hercule continued.

The manager mouse stroked his whiskers. "Well, yesterday a very **well-dressed** ratlet carrying a briefcase came by. He was wearing a **S T R O N G** cologne. The whole store smelled like cheddar-vanilla biscuits for hours after he left!"

"**Cheddar vanilla?**" I squeaked. "Just like at the jewelry store!"

Hercule nodded. "What did the ratlet want?" he asked.

"He asked our pharmacist if she had anything that would be good for his insomnia. She showed him some things, and he bought everything she suggested. He definitely seemed a little strange."

"Wait!" I squeaked, grabbing Hercule's arm. "Maybe that's why the mouseum guard slept through the heist! "Our thieves slipped him a **sleeping pill**!"

"You must be right!" Hercule agreed. "Let's head back to the mouseum."

But then I remembered the PROMISE I'd made to Trap. "First I have to buy aLMONDS for my cousin," I said. "You go to the mouseum, and I'll take care of the nuts." I grabbed a one-pound bag of aLMONDS from a nearby display and paid the manager mouse as Hercule dashed outside.

Then it was back to the Grand Hotel for me!

TRAP STILTON, SUPER CHEF

Twenty minutes—and another long bike ride!—later I was back in the New Mouse City **GRAND HOTEL** kitchen with Trap.

"Thank Gouda you're back. What took you so **long**?"

I sighed. "I am sorry, Trap. It's a **LONG** story. But here are your **ALMONDS**." I turned to go. "So, if that's all you need—"

"Of course not!" Trap interrupted, wrapping me in an apron.

Apron time!

Squeak!

"We have a chocolate egg to bake!"

"B-b-but aren't we done with the **TASTINGS**?" I stammered.

"Yes, but now I need a baking assistant!" Trap cried.

Before I could squeak out any objections, Trap popped a **CHEF'S** hat on my head. It was so big, I couldn't see the **whiskers** on the front of my **snout**.

Then Trap handed me an enormouse **recipe** book called *Eggcellent Eggs.*

"Come on, Cousin, we have a **first-prize-winning** chocolate egg to make!"

Perfect!

The book was so heavy I dropped it on the floor! I heaved it off the ground and started to flip through it. I gasped.

"Trap, this book is full of recipes that *use* eggs . . . it's not for *making* chocolate eggs! Look, there's a section on chicken eggs, one on quail eggs, duck eggs . . ." I trailed off.

My cousin turned as white as a slice of mozzarella cheese: "OH NO! What am I going to do now?" He pulled at the fur on his head.

This was a disaster. I needed to meet Hercule at the mouseum, but Trap was in BIG TROUBLE!

"It might be time to call in a master baker," I suggested.

But my cousin just shook his head. "I'm Trap Stilton. I have a baking column in the

Rodent's Gazette! We can figure this out by ourselves. It will be as easy as cheesy pie!"

I could see that there was no getting out of Trap's kitchen. I tightened the straps on my apron. The faster we got to work, the faster I could get back to Hercule!

So we got to work . . . and to guessing at the recipe!

Squeeak, it was not easy at all!

We tried a few different recipes:

The first chocolate egg leaned to the left.

The second one leaned to the right.

The third one was flat on top.

The fourth one was flat on the bottom.

The fifth one had strange spots.

The sixth one had holes like Swiss cheese.

Finally, the seventh one was . . . okay.

By the end of it, we were covered in

chocolate from snout to tail! But we had successfully made an **ENORMOUSE** chocolate egg! Well, sort of successfully . . . It looked a little lumpy.

But Trap seemed happy. "What a masterpiece!" he cried.

THE FIRST CHOCOLATE EGG LEANED TO THE LEFT.

THE THIRD ONE WAS FLAT ON TOP.

THE SECOND ONE LEANED TO THE RIGHT.

THE FOURTH ONE WAS FLAT ON THE BOTTOM.

Trap wrapped the egg with golden paper, decorated it with a **BiG BOW**, and sighed happily. "All done! Can you be a **FABUMOUSE** cousin and take it to the judging panel in the town square? I'll get everything *cleaned* up here."

"Sure, Trap," I said. The town square was near the mouseum, so I wouldn't lose much more time. I carefully picked up the CHOCOLATE egg and waved good-bye to Trap.

THE MYSTERIOUS MOUSELET

Back at my bike, I had an **unpleasant** surprise: the egg did not fit in the bike basket! I'd have to rent a trailer from the bike-share station. This bike thing was getting **EXPENSIVE**!

Once I rented the trailer and attached it to my BIKE, I started pedaling as *fast* as I could to the mouseum.

Once I arrived, Hercule met me out front with the guard who had been given the sleeping pill.

"The GUARD has remembered that

right before falling asleep, a mouselet with red hair from the food stand across the street offered him a CHEESY milkshake."

"I couldn't resist!" the guard said. "It smelled like CHEDDAR VANILLA—my favorite!

"That scent again!" I cried. "But how could there be so many suspicious mice that smelled the same? (1) A BLOND-HAIRED mouse at the museum. (2) A DARK-HAIRED rodent at the jewelry store. (3) A RED-HAIRED

mouselet with the guard!

"Don't forget the fourth—**(4)** the **ratlet** who bought the sleeping medicine at the **ORGANIC STORE** smelled like **cheddar vanilla**, too!"

"What in the name of stinky Gorgonzola does it all mean?" I wondered. Just then I caught a glimpse of the time on my

phone. "Squeak!" I cried. "I have to go! I PROMISED Trap I would drop off his entry for the baking competition!"

"All right," Geronimo," Hercule said. "I have an errand of my own to run—I'm dropping off these flowers for Thea!" He pulled an enormous BOUQUET of yellow roses out from behind his back. "See you at my office in half an hour!"

I ROLLED my eyes and hopped back on my bike. How did he have time for FLOWERS when we were so close to CRACKING the case!

FISH BONES AND ROTTEN EGGS

Once I got on my bike, I decided to head to Hercule's office first. I could drop off my bike there and walk Trap's egg to the judging station. I decided that would be **FASTER**, since by now the streets in the center of town were probably clogged with Spring Festival–going rodents.

Holey Swiss cheese, we were running out of time to find the Mousebergé Egg! The exhibition opening—and the whole Spring Festival—would be a disaster without it! I was so lost in thought about the egg that I hadn't noticed how fast I was going. Buildings whipped past me at an ever-increasing speed. I had to slow down!

I pumped the brakes—but nothing happened!

Squeak!

The trailer on the back of the bike started to careen back and forth, making it hard to steer. I had to SLOW the bike down somehow or I would end up splattered like a dropped cheese frittata, along with Trap's precious chocolate egg!

There was only one thing to do. I'd have to steer off the road now, before I picked up any more speed! I spied a garbage bin on a nearby corner and aimed right at it. I closed my eyes and hoped for the best.

Oh no!

Baaaaaang!

Gross!

I flew off my bike and

landed right inside! It was a good thing I had my helmet on . . . although it didn't protect me from the **garbage smell**.

Yuck!

When I got out of the trash, however, I smelled something mousetastic— **CHEDDAR VANILLA!**

I took my **cell phone** out to call Hercule but . . . the battery was dead! There was only one thing left to do . . . follow the **trail** of the scent on my own!

Yuck!

Even though the bike had been ruined in the CRASH, Trap's egg was miraculously unharmed. I sighed in relief and hoisted it onto my shoulders.

I followed the delicious scent of cheddar vanilla all the way to the docks. It seemed like the fabumouse smell was coming from inside a big **blue** shipping container. Quiet as a mouse, I crept close enough to peer inside.

I couldn't believe my eyes!

I recognized the mouselet inside right away—it was SHADOW, the smartest thief in all of Mouse Island! That's why each rodent's description of the thief had been so

Shadow!

different, except for the smell of cheddar-vanilla perfume! The blond mouselet, the dark-haired mouselet, the red-haired mouselet, the ratlet with the briefcase — they had all been Shadow in disguise!

I had to do something right away . . . but what? Then suddenly . . .

HONK! HONK! HOONNK!

A departing ship's horn startled me. I jumped, hitting my snout against the edge of the metallic wall. BANG!

Shadow turned around and saw me in the doorway. "Geronimo Stilton? Is that you?"

I rubbed my SORE snout. "Hands up, Shadow! You are under arrest!"

Shadow burst out **laughing**. "You can't stop me, Stilton. As soon as they load this container on my ship, I will be safely headed to the South Seas! And the Spring

Festival will be ruined!"

Was this all about the festival and not just the priceless Mousebergé Egg? "Why would you want to **RUiN** the Spring Festival?" I asked.

"The Spring Festival is a **SILLY** tradition," she cried, her eyes flashing. "No one ever gives me a chocolate egg. It isn't fair." She paused and an **evil** grin spread across her snout. "If I can't enjoy the Spring Festival, then no one can!"

I shook my head in **DISBELIEF**.

"That's why I'm stealing the Mousebergé Egg. "It's more beautiful than any chocolate egg, and taking it will ruin everyone else's **fun**, too!"

This was a cat-astrophe!

But suddenly I had an idea.

"Here," I said, handing her Trap's **CHOCOLATE** egg. "I would like you to have this chocolate egg. It might not be the most beautiful or the best-tasting **chocolate** egg in the world, but Trap and I baked it together."

Shadow looked suspicious. "Why are you giving it to me?"

Here, this is for you!

Why?

"Because I believe every rodent deserves a **second chance** . . . and a Spring Festival chocolate egg! Come to the mouseum with me. You could return the Mouseberge Egg yourself and see how cheddariffic the festival can be!"

Shadow took the chocolate egg. I could see that she was considering my suggestion.

Suddenly, the shipping container moved and everything around us started shaking! I staggered to the door and looked out to see the ground speeding away from us.

"The crane is loading the container on the ship!" I cried.

The container tilted to one side, and I grabbed at the doorframe, terrified. One wrong move and I was *cheese toast*!

"HELPPPP!"

Shadow's PAW grabbed me just in time

and pulled me to safety!

Squeeeak! I was safe, but . . . I couldn't help it, I fainted from fear.

When I came to and opened my eyes, I was safely back on the ***dock***. But there was no sign of the shipping container, or of SHADOW.

I hurried to my feet and squinted at a ship that was rumbling out to sea. I caught a glimpse of blond hair before the ship turned and steamed out into the ocean.

Rats! Shadow had gotten away again!

But then a golden glimmer caught my eye.

THE MOUSEBERGÉ EGG!

Shadow had decided to return it after all. The *Spring Festival* was saved!

A GOOD EGG

I grabbed the very Precious Mouseberegé Egg, got a new bicycle at a BIKE-SHARE station, and headed for Hercule's office, pedaling as fast as I could. But he wasn't there! *He must be back at the mouseum,* I thought. *Time to ride like my tail is on* FIRE*!*

When I pulled up to the front of the mouseum, I saw that my hunch had been correct. Hercule ran toward me.

"When you didn't show up at the office, I got worried and came back to the mouseum," he cried. His snout dropped open when he saw what I was holding in my paws. "GREAT BALLS OF MOZZARELLA, you found the Mouseberegé Egg! That's incredimouse!"

I stowed my bike and we dashed into the mouseum's main hall.

Grant von Paintmouse rushed to put the Mousebergé Egg back where it belonged and threw open the **mouseum** doors to the public.

It seemed like all of New Mouse City was there for the exhibit opening. The rodents were happy to be able to admire such a masterpiece. Every mouse was having a wonderful time, except me.

"What's wrong, Geronimo?" Hercule asked, noting my **worried** expression.

"I gave Trap's chocolate egg to Shadow in order to get her to return the

TIPPY

AUNT SWEETFUR

UNCLE GRAYFUR

MOUSELLA

ALYSSA
SWEETFEET

Mousebergé Egg. Now he'll have nothing to enter in the baking competition and it's all my fault!" I put my face in my paws. "Trap will be so disappointed."

But just then I felt a GENTLE tug on my jacket sleeve.

It was my BELOVED nephew Benjamin! "Uncle, I heard what you said . . . don't worry, there's still time to replace the egg!"

"I don't think so, Benjamin. The first egg took us HOURS

THEA

BRUCE HYENA

MR. FRITTATA

BENJAMIN

MS. FETA

GRANDPA WILLIAM

AUNT SUGARFUR

UNCLE KINDPAWS

to make," I said sadly.

"I have a plan. The first egg took you hours because there were only two of you doing all the work. I believe if we round up a bunch of mice, we can re-create it in no time!" Benjamin said.

My ears perked up. "You might be onto something," I cried. "Let's try it! Call as many rodents as you can and let's all meet in my kitchen!"

NUTTY CHOCORAT

FONDUE

FONTINA

READY, SET, BAKE!

One after the other, ALL my friends and relatives showed up at my house. The first to arrive was Trap.

"I don't know about this. I don't THINK anyone will be able to top my original egg!" he grumbled.

Then Aunt Sweetfur, Grandpa William, Bruce Hyena, Thea, and Hercule arrived.

Mousella walked in next, followed by all my Rodent's Gazette colleagues.

"Mr. Stilton, I stopped on the way and picked up cocoa powder!" she said.

Everymouse had brought something to contribute: pots, molds, spatulas, sugar, rare spices, candy, honey, marzipan, glazed decorations.

CANDIED FRUIT

MARZIPAN

SPATULAS

COCOA

What fabumouse friends!
What a mouserific family!
What a lucky ratlet I am!

Once everyone was there, Benjamin turned to me. "Well, **UNCLE**, tell us what to do!"

I cleared my throat. "Friends, thank you for being here! **Trap and I are very grateful for your help.** You all know Nutty Chocorat, right?"

CANDY

SPICES

POTS

FLOUR

MOLDS

HONEY

MILK

PASTRY BRUSH

Everyone nodded.

"He will **take the lead** and show us how to bake a mouserific **chocolate** egg!" I cried. Upon hearing this news, everyone enthusiastically clapped their paws together.

Nutty Chocorat stepped forward. "Together we will bake the best chocolate egg in town—in record time! *Are you ready?*"

"Yessssss!" we all cried together

"Then, let's get *going*!" Nutty Chocorat said.

Everymouse got to work measuring, chopping, and baking. In no time, we had created an **ENORMOUSE, COLORFUL, DELICIOUS, CHOCOLATE EGG!**"

Nutty Chocorat is the most famouse chocolate expert on Mouse Island.

"That's the most **FABUMOUSE** egg I've ever seen!" I cried.

Next to me, Trap snorted. "After mine, of course," he mumbled. But he looked pleased with the new egg.

"Since we all baked this egg together," I said, "we should call it THE GREAT FRIENDSHIP EGG!"

As Sweet as Friendship!

We took the egg to the contest judging station, and we made it *just in time*!

I could tell that our egg immediately **impressed** the judges. The MULTICOLORED decorations really made it stand out. Nutty Chocorat had even written *The Great Friendship Egg* on the front in beautiful script.

The judges walked all around it, admiring

Woo-hoo!   Let's go!   It's beautiful!   Yay!   Hurry!

the outside, and then sliced into it so they could have a taste. I saw one judge go back for a S E C O N D helping.

Then they gathered in a huddle, comparing notes on all the incredimouse eggs they had tasted that day.

After what seemed like forever, the judges finally returned to the stage to declare a winner.

"And now, the moment you've all been waiting for," the head judge said.

Team Stilton gathered by the stage, and we held each other's paws. Did we have a chance?

"The WINNER of the Spring Festival baking competition is . . ." the head judge started. "The Great Friendship Egg, baked by Trap Stilton and friends!"

The audience clapped and we swarmed

around Trap to offer congratulatory hugs.

"I've done it!" Trap cheered. "But, of course, I couldn't have done it without the help of all of my FABUMOUSE friends," Trap said. "And my incredimouse cousin Geronimo Stilton."

The Mousebergé Egg was back where it belonged. I had a MOUSERIFFIC story to tell in the *Rodent's Gazette* Spring Festival special issue, Trap had won the baking competition—and I was surrounded by all my favorite rodents. This had been the BEST Spring Festival ever!

"Enough talking!" I cried.

"Let's eat this chocolate egg!"

Be sure to read all my fabumouse adventures!

#1 Lost Treasure of the Emerald Eye

#2 The Curse of the Cheese Pyramid

#3 Cat and Mouse in a Haunted House

#4 I'm Too Fond of My Fur!

#5 Four Mice Deep in the Jungle

#6 Paws Off, Cheddarface!

#7 Red Pizzas for a Blue Count

#8 Attack of the Bandit Cats

#9 A Fabumouse Vacation for Geronimo

#10 All Because of a Cup of Coffee

#11 It's Halloween, You 'Fraidy Mouse!

#12 Merry Christmas, Geronimo!

#13 The Phantom of the Subway

#14 The Temple of the Ruby of Fire

#15 The Mona Mousa Code

#16 A Cheese-Colored Camper

#17 Watch Your Whiskers, Stilton!

#18 Shipwreck on the Pirate Islands

#19 My Name Is Stilton, Geronimo Stilton

#20 Surf's Up, Geronimo!

#21 The Wild, Wild West

#22 The Secret of Cacklefur Castle

A Christmas Tale

#23 Valentine's Day Disaster

#24 Field Trip to Niagara Falls

#25 The Search for Sunken Treasure

#26 The Mummy with No Name

#27 The Christmas Toy Factory

#28 Wedding Crasher

#29 Down and Out Down Under

#30 The Mouse Island Marathon

#31 The Mysterious Cheese Thief

Christmas Catastrophe

#32 Valley of the Giant Skeletons

#33 Geronimo and the Gold Medal Mystery

#34 Geronimo Stilton, Secret Agent

#35 A Very Merry Christmas

#36 Geronimo's Valentine

#37 The Race Across America

#38 A Fabumouse School Adventure

#39 Singing Sensation

#40 The Karate Mouse

#41 Mighty Mount Kilimanjaro

#42 The Peculiar Pumpkin Thief

#43 I'm Not a Supermouse!

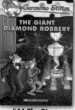
#44 The Giant Diamond Robbery

#45 Save the White Whale!

#46 The Haunted Castle

#47 Run for the Hills,
Geronimo!

#48 The Mystery in
Venice

#49 The Way of
the Samurai

#50 This Hotel Is
Haunted!

#51 The Enormouse
Pearl Heist

#52 Mouse in Space!

#53 Rumble in
the Jungle

#54 Get into Gear,
Stilton!

#55 The Golden
Statue Plot

#56 Flight of the
Red Bandit

The Hunt for the
Golden Book

#57 The Stinky
Cheese Vacation

#58 The Super
Chef Contest

#59 Welcome to
Moldy Manor

The Hunt for the
Curious Cheese

#60 The Treasure of
Easter Island

#61 Mouse House
Hunter

#62 Mouse
Overboard!

The Hunt for the
Secret Papyrus

#63 The Cheese
Experiment

#64 Magical Mission

#65 Bollywood
Burglary

The Hunt for the
Hundredth Key

#66 Operation:
Secret Recipe

#67 The Chocolate
Chase

MEET
Geronimo Stiltonord

He is a mouseking — the Geronimo Stilton of the ancient far north! He lives with his brawny and brave clan in the village of Mouseborg. From sailing frozen waters to facing fiery dragons, every day is an adventure for the micekings!

#1 Attack of the Dragons

#2 The Famouse Fjord Race

#3 Pull the Dragon's Tooth!

#4 Stay Strong, Geronimo!

#5 The Mysterious Message

#6 The Helmet Holdup

Don't miss any of these exciting Thea Sisters adventures!

Thea Stilton and the
Dragon's Code

Thea Stilton and the
Mountain of Fire

Thea Stilton and the
Ghost of the Shipwreck

Thea Stilton and the
Secret City

Thea Stilton and the
Mystery in Paris

Thea Stilton and the
Cherry Blossom Adventure

Thea Stilton and the
Star Castaways

Thea Stilton: Big Trouble
in the Big Apple

Thea Stilton and the
Ice Treasure

Thea Stilton and the
Secret of the Old Castle

Thea Stilton and the
Blue Scarab Hunt

Thea Stilton and the
Prince's Emerald

Thea Stilton and the
Mystery on the Orient Express

Thea Stilton and the
Dancing Shadows

Thea Stilton and the
Legend of the Fire Flowers

Thea Stilton and the
Spanish Dance Mission

Thea Stilton and the
Journey to the Lion's Den

Thea Stilton and the Great Tulip Heist

Thea Stilton and the Chocolate Sabotage

Thea Stilton and the Missing Myth

Thea Stilton and the Lost Letters

Thea Stilton and the Tropical Treasure

Thea Stilton and the Hollywood Hoax

Thea Stilton and the Madagascar Madness

Thea Stilton and the Frozen Fiasco

And check out my fabumouse special editions!

THEA STILTON: THE JOURNEY TO ATLANTIS

THEA STILTON: THE SECRET OF THE FAIRIES

THEA STILTON: THE SECRET OF THE SNOW

THEA STILTON: THE CLOUD CASTLE

THEA STILTON: THE TREASURE OF THE SEA

Don't miss any of my special edition adventures!

THE KINGDOM OF FANTASY

THE QUEST FOR PARADISE:
THE RETURN TO THE KINGDOM OF FANTASY

THE AMAZING VOYAGE:
THE THIRD ADVENTURE IN THE KINGDOM OF FANTASY

THE DRAGON PROPHECY:
THE FOURTH ADVENTURE IN THE KINGDOM OF FANTASY

THE VOLCANO OF FIRE:
THE FIFTH ADVENTURE IN THE KINGDOM OF FANTASY

THE SEARCH FOR TREASURE:
THE SIXTH ADVENTURE IN THE KINGDOM OF FANTASY

THE ENCHANTED CHARMS:
THE SEVENTH ADVENTURE IN THE KINGDOM OF FANTASY

THE PHOENIX OF DESTINY:
AN EPIC KINGDOM OF FANTASY ADVENTURE

THE HOUR OF MAGIC:
THE EIGHTH ADVENTURE IN THE KINGDOM OF FANTASY

THE WIZARD'S WAND:
THE NINTH ADVENTURE IN THE KINGDOM OF FANTASY

THE SHIP OF SECRETS:
THE TENTH ADVENTURE IN THE KINGDOM OF FANTASY

THE DRAGON OF FORTUNE:
AN EPIC KINGDOM OF FANTASY ADVENTURE

THE JOURNEY THROUGH TIME

BACK IN TIME:
THE SECOND JOURNEY THROUGH TIME

THE RACE AGAINST TIME:
THE THIRD JOURNEY THROUGH TIME

LOST IN TIME:
THE FOURTH JOURNEY THROUGH TIME

MEET
GERONIMO STILTONIX

He is a spacemouse — the Geronimo Stilton of a parallel universe! He is captain of the spaceship *MouseStar 1*. While flying through the cosmos, he visits distant planets and meets crazy aliens. His adventures are out of this world!

#1 Alien Escape

#2 You're Mine, Captain!

#3 Ice Planet Adventure

#4 The Galactic Goal

#5 Rescue Rebellion

#6 The Underwater Planet

#7 Beware! Space Junk!

#8 Away in a Star Sled

#9 Slurp Monster Showdown

#10 Pirate Spacecat Attack

#11 We'll Bite Your Tail, Geronimo!

ABOUT THE AUTHOR

Born in New Mouse City, Mouse Island, **GERONIMO STILTON** is Rattus Emeritus of Mousomorphic Literature and of Neo-Ratonic Comparative Philosophy. For the past twenty years, he has been running *The Rodent's Gazette,* New Mouse City's most widely read daily newspaper.

Stilton was awarded the Ratitzer Prize for his scoops on *The Curse of the Cheese Pyramid* and *The Search for Sunken Treasure.* He has also received the Andersen 2000 Prize for Personality of the Year. One of his bestsellers won the 2002 eBook Award for world's best ratlings' electronic book. His works have been published all over the globe.

In his spare time, Mr. Stilton collects antique cheese rinds and plays golf. But what he most enjoys is telling stories to his nephew Benjamin.

1. Main entrance
2. Printing presses (where the books and newspaper are printed)
3. Accounts department
4. Editorial room (where the editors, illustrators, and designers work)
5. Geronimo Stilton's office
6. Helicopter landing pad

THE RODENT'S GAZETTE

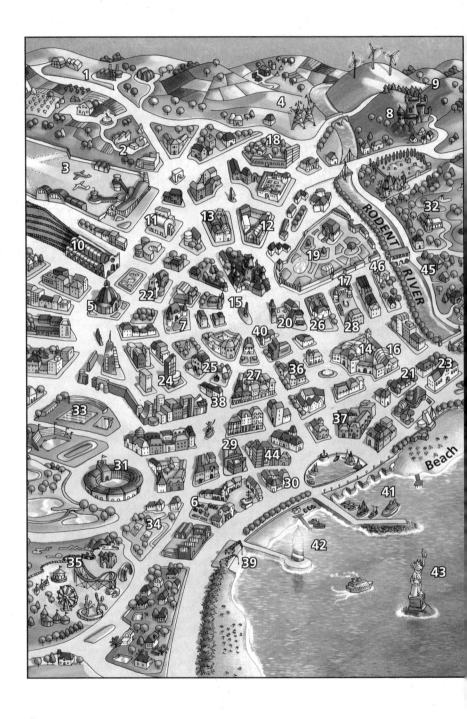

Map of New Mouse City

1. Industrial Zone
2. Cheese Factories
3. Angorat International Airport
4. WRAT Radio and Television Station
5. Cheese Market
6. Fish Market
7. Town Hall
8. Snotnose Castle
9. The Seven Hills of Mouse Island
10. Mouse Central Station
11. Trade Center
12. Movie Theater
13. Gym
14. Catnegie Hall
15. Singing Stone Plaza
16. The Gouda Theater
17. Grand Hotel
18. Mouse General Hospital
19. Botanical Gardens
20. Cheap Junk for Less (Trap's store)
21. Aunt Sweetfur and Benjamin's House
22. Mouseum of Modern Art
23. University and Library
24. *The Daily Rat*
25. *The Rodent's Gazette*
26. Trap's House
27. Fashion District
28. The Mouse House Restaurant
29. Environmental Protection Center
30. Harbor Office
31. Mousidon Square Garden
32. Golf Course
33. Swimming Pool
34. Tennis Courts
35. Curlyfur Island Amousement Park
36. Geronimo's House
37. Historic District
38. Public Library
39. Shipyard
40. Thea's House
41. New Mouse Harbor
42. Luna Lighthouse
43. The Statue of Liberty
44. Hercule Poirat's Office
45. Petunia Pretty Paws's House
46. Grandfather William's House

Map of Mouse Island

1. Big Ice Lake
2. Frozen Fur Peak
3. Slipperyslopes Glacier
4. Coldcreeps Peak
5. Ratzikistan
6. Transratania
7. Mount Vamp
8. Roastedrat Volcano
9. Brimstone Lake
10. Poopedcat Pass
11. Stinko Peak
12. Dark Forest
13. Vain Vampires Valley
14. Goose Bumps Gorge
15. The Shadow Line Pass
16. Penny Pincher Castle
17. Nature Reserve Park
18. Las Ratayas Marinas
19. Fossil Forest
20. Lake Lake

21. Lake Lakelake
22. Lake Lakelakelake
23. Cheddar Crag
24. Cannycat Castle
25. Valley of the Giant Sequoia
26. Cheddar Springs
27. Sulfurous Swamp
28. Old Reliable Geyser
29. Vole Vale
30. Ravingrat Ravine
31. Gnat Marshes
32. Munster Highlands
33. Mousehara Desert
34. Oasis of the Sweaty Camel
35. Cabbagehead Hill
36. Rattytrap Jungle
37. Rio Mosquito

Dear mouse friends,
Thanks for reading, and farewell
till the next book.
It'll be another whisker-licking-good
adventure, and that's a promise!

Geronimo Stilton